THE GOAT LADY

by Jane Bregoli

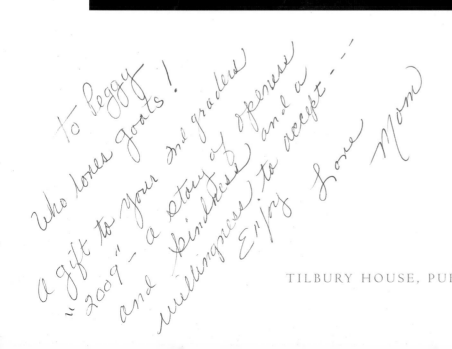

TILBURY HOUSE, PUBLISHERS · GARDINER, MAINE

From the day we moved into our new home, we were fascinated by a nearby farmhouse. Most of the homes in our neighborhood were new, freshly painted, with neatly mowed lawns, but the old farm-house on the corner of Lucy Little Road was different from the others. That house's paint was peeling, its doors hung crookedly from their hinges, and the yard was full of white goats. We liked to watch the frisky baby goats. They pranced up the porch steps, hopped onto rusty barrels, and even jumped onto their mothers' backs!

We wondered who took care of the goats. Men in a truck delivered hay, a lady came with groceries, a van appeared each weekday at noon. Sometimes a big yellow school bus was parked by the gate. We watched for lights in the windows at night. Occasionally a glimmer of light shone through a torn green window shade early in the evening— but the house was dark before our bedtime.

There was a lot of talk in our neighborhood about the goats' mysterious owner. Mom heard complaints about the unkempt yard, the rundown house, and the unruly animals.

"That big gray goose chased me again on my way to get the mail," moaned the man who jogged by with a radio set on his head.

"That rooster crows day and night, and the chickens are always in the street," grumbled the salesman who lived next door.

"Those goats keep hopping over their fence and coming into my yard. They ate the new apple tree I just planted," complained the history teacher who lived across the street.

Finally one cold October day we saw her—a slightly bent, but still rather tall woman was feeding the hungry herd of goats. Cautiously, we picked our way through rocks and weeds toward her. The goats bleated to their owner between mouthfuls of hay. Around our feet chickens were busy pecking the ground for bits of grain the goats had dropped. The big gray goose came running toward us, honking a loud warning. We stood there bravely.

"Have you come to see the goats?" the goat lady asked. She was dressed warmly but none of her clothes matched. Her coat was held closed with a piece of twine to make up for missing buttons.

My fears quickly disappeared when I saw the way her eyes twinkled and the warm smile between her rosy cheeks. She introduced herself with a hint of an accent, "I am Noelie Lemire Houle, French Canadian, born in 1899."

Then she called out, "Anna, come here, Anna!"

A goat with a black mark on her face the size of a quarter bleated m-a-a-a and scampered across the field to be petted. Noelie gave her a snack she had in her pocket.

"Goats will answer to their names if you treat them kindly," she said. She pointed out Darcey, Dottie, Elaine, June, and Vincent, as well as their brothers and sisters. She proudly told us that many of her goats had won ribbons at the county fairs.

"Goats are clean animals," she explained while I petted the gentle Anna. "They don't eat tin cans or garbage—but see how they've nibbled at the corners of my house?"

Then we heard our mother's call, and it was time to leave. Noelie invited us to come again, anytime. We ran home full of excitement, with lots to tell our mom. We were happy to have finally met Noelie and her goats!

The very next afternoon we returned to the farm to help Noelie with chores. We learned that goats need fresh water each day. We helped feed them dried corn and grain and hay. The curious goats nibbled at my jacket pocket, where I had some bread I had brought just for Anna.

When it was time to milk, Noelie took a piece of twine from a hay bale and used it to lead a goat to the milking stand in the barn. She sat on a stool, gently resting her head against the goat's warm side, and hummed a tune from one of her favorite operas while she milked. Slowly and steadily the milk began to fill the pail while the goat listened to Noelie's comforting song.

Noelie taught me to milk, too. It was harder than it looked. We saved the cream that rose to the top of the milk for her coffee.

On rainy days we fed the goats in the red barn they shared with the chickens and ducks and the big gray goose. A still-bright oriental rug hung in the barn's doorway, serving as a door to keep the wind out.

"Most people think that animals can stand all kinds of weather," Noelie told us in a concerned voice. "But if you have animals you should sleep in the barn yourself one night. If it isn't comfortable for you, then it isn't comfortable for them."

We visited Noelie often that winter and liked helping her with the friendly goats. One day Anna didn't want to eat. Noelie put her in the kidding pen, hinting with a wink of her eye, "Maybe there will be a surprise tomorrow." In the morning there were three snow-white baby goats with Anna! I got to name them—Kaylyn, Peggy, and Joan. I liked them best, and they quickly learned to follow me around when I visited the farm.

One of Noelie's favorite sayings was, "The goats are my kids," because she didn't have any children of her own. If any of the new baby goats were sick or weak, she whisked them right into the house to be nursed back to health. I helped feed them goat formula from a baby bottle with a long nipple. They napped on blankets and nibbled at the big bags of goat feed. Being mountain goats, they climbed on top of whatever they could.

In warm weather the doors and windows of Noelie's house were always open, allowing the goats to roam in and out freely. There were no screens on the doors or windows—"So the flies and mosquitoes can escape," Noelie would say.

The neighbors talked endlessly about the goats in Noelie's house. "How many are there now?" they asked us. Some of them even reported Noelie to the town officials. They said the animals were a public nuisance. Of course we didn't agree.

Besides goats, Noelie's kitchen had an old-fashioned clothes washer. We had never seen one like it. Noelie hung her clean laundry out on a clothesline between her house and a pole across the yard. One piece always remained on the line—a white handkerchief. I reminded her one day that she had forgotten it and she laughed, saying, "It's showing me which way the wind is blowing. That helps me know what the weather is going to do."

After the goats had been fed, Noelie liked to sit at the big table in the middle of her kitchen where she listened to the radio or read a newspaper with a magnifying glass. Sometimes we gathered around the table and Noelie read *Heidi* out loud to us.

I also liked the times when Noelie told us about her own life. She had many stories, having lived almost a century. She had grown up in Canada but came to our country when she was a young woman to work in a factory.

One day I asked her why she had so many goats.

"Many years ago I became ill with arthritis," she said quietly. "My bones ached so much that I could hardly walk. I had to quit my job. There was no medicine to help me, but the doctor suggested I try drinking goat's milk. So I bought my first goat and called her Girl. I could barely walk to the barn. My hands hurt so much when I tried to milk her that I cried. Girl turned around and licked the tears off my face because she knew I was suffering."

"I drank goat's milk every day and every night. Within months I felt much better. I was so happy to feel well again, I began to raise more goats so that other people could be helped by drinking their milk. At one time I had as many as seventy-nine goats, and people started calling me the 'Goat Lady.' People used to come from far away to get the milk. There were always more

people than there was milk," she told us with a sparkle in her eye.

"Every year more goat kids were born. There wasn't room for them all, so when they were old enough I gave them to an organization that sent them to people in poor countries, so that those people would have fresh milk to drink, too."

Noelie had become a very special person to us, and one day I asked our mom if she would like to paint a portrait of Noelie and her goats. Mom is an artist who likes to paint portraits of people. She thought it was a wonderful idea and asked Noelie to pose for her.

"Who wants to see pictures of me?" Noelie laughed. "I'm an old woman, I'm over ninety years old, and I've never been a fashionable dresser."

But Noelie agreed to pose for a painting.

While Mom was busy with her brushes and paints, Noelie sang, or the two of them talked about politics and things that were happening in the world. I liked to sit nearby, watching and listening.

After Mom finished one painting, she started another. And then another.

Noelie was so pleased with the paintings Mom did!

Mom finished enough paintings of Noelie and her goats to fill the walls of the town hall for an art show. On opening night of the show, lots of people came: the "Meals on Wheels" drivers who brought Noelie's lunch on weekdays; the young man who helped her feed the goats between his school bus runs; the church lady who helped her with grocery shopping; the men who delivered hay and dried corn; the nurse who changed the bandage on her sore leg; the nurse's husband, who liked to talk in French with Noelie; and a young woman who had been able to drink only goat's milk when she was a child.

Word got out about the art show and more and more people came. After seeing Mom's beautiful paintings, the neighbors became more accepting of Noelie's way of life. The yard didn't seem quite as messy, the old house didn't look so rundown, and the animals didn't appear to be as unruly as before.

The jogger knew her name now and said, "Noelie is such a nice woman." He started bringing bread scraps for the big gray goose.

The salesman asked Noelie about getting some chickens of his own.

The history teacher offered to help fix her fence.

The town selectmen even surprised Noelie with an award for providing the citizens of our town with fresh goat's milk for so many years and asked her to ride in a limousine at the head of the Fourth of July parade!

Despite her new fame, Noelie's life remained the same as before—humble,

simple, and plain. The care of her goats was the most important thing in her life.

As Noelie got older, my mom and other friends helped more with the chores.

We did, too. When Noelie could no longer care for her goats, she arranged for them to go to a nearby farm where they could stay together as a family with the chickens, ducks, and the big gray goose.

I still love to look at the paintings of Noelie. I look beyond the wrinkles in her face and the old clothes she wore fastened with baling twine. The paintings show so much more about the Goat Lady. They show her courage and her kindness, most of all.

TILBURY HOUSE, PUBLISHERS
103 Brunswick Avenue, Gardiner, ME 04345
800–582–1899 • www.tilburyhouse.com

First hardcover printing: October 2004 • 10 9 8 7 6 4 3
First paperback printing: August 2008 • 10 9 8 7 6 5 4 3 2 1

Dedication—

To my mother Dorothy, who always encouraged me to be a painter, and to my children David and Jessica, who have shared this journey with me. —J. B.

Library of Congress Cataloging-in-Publication Data
Bregoli, Jane, 1952-
    The Goat Lady / Jane Bregoli.
        p. cm.
Summary: Tells the story of an elderly French-Canadian woman who lived in Massachusetts and raised goats
to provide milk for people who needed it.
    ISBN 0-88448-260-X (alk. paper)
    1. Houle, Noelie Lemire, b. 1899—Juvenile literature. 2. Goat farmers—Massachusetts—Dartmouth—
Biography—Juvenile literature. 3. Dartmouth (Mass.)—Biography—juvenile literature. [1. Houle, Noelie Lemire,
b. 1899. 2. Goats. 3. Old age.] I. Title.
    CT275.H64714 B74 2004
    759.13—dc22   2003018076

Noelie Lemire Houle was born in 1899 on a small farm in Quebec, Canada. She moved to the United States in 1919 to join an older sister and take a job in a corset factory in Massachusetts. When she married Almador Houle, they lived with his parents in a small farmhouse in Dartmouth, which they later inherited along with the surrounding land. Noelie and Almador worked in an electronics factory for many years. When Almador became ill, they had to sell off pieces of their land to pay his medical bills, and new houses were built nearby. After Almador's death, Noelie remained on the now-tiny farm with her goats, selling goat's milk, cheese, eggs, and honey.

Noelie gave her extra goat kids to Heifer International, a non-profit organization. Since 1944 Heifer International has helped more than 5 million hungry families in approximately 125 countries move toward self-reliance through the gift of livestock and training. You can learn more about their work at www.heifer.org.

Designed by Geraldine Millham, Westport, MA.
Editing and production by Jennifer Bunting, Audrey Maynard, and Barbara Diamond.
Color scans, printing, and binding by Sung In, South Korea.